D0445235

by Perdita Finn

Little, Brown and Company
New York ★ Boston

Little, Brown and Company

Hachette Book Group
1290 Avenue of the Americas, New York, NY 10104
Visit us at lb-kids.com

Little, Brown and Company is a division of Hachette Book Group, Inc.
The Little, Brown name and logo are trademarks of Hachette Book Group, Inc.

The publisher is not responsible for websites (or their content)
that are not owned by the publisher.

First Edition: October 2015

Library of Congress Control Number: 2015940642

ISBN 978-0-316-41080-9

10 9 8 7 6 5 4 3 2

RRD-C

Printed in the United States of America

For Audrey D. and her grandma,
Some of my very best friends

CONTENTS

✶ ✶ ✶

CHAPTER

1

A Whole New Ball Game

* * *

Sunset Shimmer dashed toward Canterlot High. Her red-gold hair wafted behind her like a pony's wavy mane. She was so excited! She glanced at her phone one more time. Could the news really be true?

She ran over to the statue of the Wondercolt. Rainbow Dash and Applejack were already there, and the other girls were seconds behind her. "I got your text, Rainbow Dash," Sunset Shimmer exclaimed breathlessly. "Did something come through the portal? Is Equestrian magic on the loose? Did Twilight come back with a problem that only we can solve?"

Pinkie Pie giggled. "Has a giant cake monster covered all the cakes in the world in cake?"

Rainbow Dash was surprised that all the girls had overreacted. What did they want? Another trio of evil Sirens to infiltrate their school and try to sow disharmony? She held up her guitar. The emergency was that she had broken a string—and she really wanted to practice some new songs for their band, the Sonic Rainbooms.

Sunset Shimmer wrinkled her forehead. "I don't understand."

"I was just telling Rainbow Dash here"—Applejack sighed—"that a broken guitar string doesn't really qualify as an emergency."

"It totally does!" Rainbow Dash couldn't believe that Applejack, who played the bass, didn't get it.

But no one did.

Rarity was put out. "Really, Rainbow Dash, I was in the middle of sewing a very complex appliqué on my latest frock."

"And I was just about to tuck in my pets at the shelter. Now we'll have to start stories all over again." Even gentle Fluttershy was annoyed.

Something just didn't seem right, but Sunset Shimmer couldn't figure out what it was. "Why would you send all of us an emergency text for a guitar string?"

Rainbow Dash whirled around and pointed at a trio of girls sitting on the school steps. Apple Bloom, Sweetie Belle, and Scootaloo were all looking at the Rainbooms expectantly.

"Fans!" explained Rainbow Dash. "I was going to show our fans some awesome guitar licks, but I kinda need all six strings to do that. Got any extra?"

Rarity rolled her eyes. Fluttershy shook her head. Pinkie Pie threw up her hands, and Applejack turned out her pockets. They were empty. But Sunset Shimmer was always prepared. She rummaged through her backpack and pulled out an extra set of strings for Rainbow Dash.

She handed them to her fellow guitar

player. "But I'm pretty sure the music rooms are locked now. It's the end of the day after all."

"No problem!" said Rainbow Dash. She restrung her guitar and gave it a triumphant strum. "The acoustics in the hallway are perfect for power chords. C'mon, let's go!"

"You coming, Sunset?" Applejack asked.

"I'll catch up in a bit," answered Sunset Shimmer.

The girls followed Rainbow Dash into the school while Sunset Shimmer looked up at the pony statue, disappointed. It was a portal to Equestria, but she had no idea when it would open again. She loved her new friends at Canterlot High, but sometimes she really missed Twilight Sparkle. When would they see her again?

Sunset Shimmer took out her magic

journal. When she wrote in it, Twilight Sparkle could read her letter in Equestria. Sunset Shimmer was so busy writing that she didn't pay any attention to the yellow bus rolling to a stop in front of the school. She didn't notice when the doors slid open and a dark-hooded figure slunk out and slipped between the shadows to the statue.

The shadowy figure removed an electronic device that began emitting high-pitched beeps. For a moment, Sunset Shimmer looked up. What was that? But it was probably just feedback from Rainbow Dash's guitar.

A needle spun wildly on the strange device and pointed directly at the Wondercolt statue.

Sunset Shimmer read over what she had written.

Dear Princess Twilight,

How's life treating you in Equestria? Any cool new magic spells? It's been pretty quiet here at CHS since the Battle of the Bands. We still pony up when we play music, which Rainbow Dash just loves to show off, but I still can't quite grasp what it's all about. I would love to hear what you think about it when you have a sec.

Your friend, Sunset Shimmer

Sunset Shimmer closed the journal and went to put it back in her backpack. But why was the Wondercolt glowing? Was the portal opening? How strange! That's when Sunset Shimmer saw the hooded figure slinking into the shadows. "Hey!" she called.

Startled, the figure pointed the strange device right at Sunset Shimmer—and it went wild, beeping and buzzing and glowing. The figure shoved the device into a pocket and took off running.

"Hey!" Sunset Shimmer shouted. "Wait! Stop!"

Sunset Shimmer raced after the hooded stranger, but the person managed to cross the street just as the light changed and traffic streamed across the road. A car honked its horn as Sunset Shimmer stepped from the curb. A bus pulled up. Sunset Shimmer saw the hooded figure peeking out from one of the windows. Too late!

"Who was that?" she wondered out loud. And what were they up to? Sunset Shimmer was worried—but she was also a little bit excited. Could a magic adventure be about to begin?

CHAPTER

2

The Name of the game

★ ★ ★

Once the bus was far away from Canterlot High, the girl pulled down her hood and shook free a mane of dark purple hair streaked with pink. It was Twilight Sparkle—the very girl who shared a name with the famous pony from Equestria. Unlike the Princess of Friendship, however, she wore glasses and she didn't seem to have a lot of friends. She was all by herself on the bus.

The bus pulled up in front of an ivy-covered brick building. A sign above the door said CRYSTAL PREP ACADEMY. Twilight hopped off the bus, bounded through the front door, and headed toward a science lab. She took her strange beeping device out of her pocket. She plugged it into an enormous computer. Lights flashed, the hard drive whirred, and the device started to glow. A printer spit out a long series of sheets. Twilight studied them carefully while a ball of light traveled from the device along a series of wires and cables to a small table in the middle of the lab.

On the table was a glass dome, and under the dome was another, smaller elec-tronic device. It snapped open like an old-fashioned phone and sucked the ball of energy into itself.

Twilight checked off something on her clipboard, satisfied. It was working, whatever it was.

Twilight powered down the computer. She lifted the glass dome and removed the new device. Behind her was a bulletin board, and on the bulletin board were photos—of all the Equestria Girls.

The Only Game in Town

★ ★ ★

The girls clustered in the library of Canterlot High the next morning, trying to figure out what was going on.

Sunset Shimmer was reviewing the facts. "They were definitely doing *something* to the statue, or were going to."

"Do you think they came through the portal from Equestria?" wondered Fluttershy.

Sunset Shimmer shook her head. "No, I'm pretty sure I would have noticed that. I think they were from over here in the human world."

Applejack sat down at a table, relieved. "Well, that's the last thing we need— another magical so-and-so bent on world domination coming over from Equestria."

Sunset Shimmer looked down at her feet, embarrassed. She had proved to the girls time and again that she had reformed and was on their side, but she always knew that they hadn't forgotten that once she had turned into a she-devil set on ruling all of Canterlot High.

Rarity broke the awkward silence. "I,

for one, have no interest in another fight against the powers of evil magic. The wear and tear on my wardrobe is just too much to keep up with."

"Still," said Sunset Shimmer, unable to hide her excitement, "a mysterious figure snooping around the portal? Don't you want to know what they are up to?"

"I don't even want to guess," said Fluttershy, worried.

"Well, you don't have to," Rainbow Dash announced. "I've totally figured out who it was." She led the girls over to the sports books in the library.

Pinkie Pie clapped her hands. "A nighttime statue cleaner? A magical portal maintenance maintainer? Ooooh! A gardener?"

Rainbow Dash shook her head. "Seeing

as how they got off a bus from the city and got back on a bus headed to the city, I'll bet they go to …"

"Crystal Prep." Everyone but Sunset Shimmer spoke the dreaded words out loud.

"Yep." Rainbow Dash nodded her head, resigned. "With the Friendship Games starting tomorrow, they'd totally try to prank us by defacing the Wondercolt statue."

Sunset Shimmer wasn't convinced. Something wasn't quite right. "Why would anyone take a bus all the way from the city for that?"

"Because," explained Applejack, "that's just what the students at Crystal Prep would do."

Rainbow Dash pulled a big volume of school sports records from the shelf. She flipped through the pages, showing the girls photo after photo of teams holding giant trophies—all wearing the uniforms of the Crystal Prep Shadowbolts. Not a single picture showed a student from Canterlot High holding a trophy.

Rainbow Dash looked dejected. "Because even though the Shadowbolts beat us in everything: soccer, tennis, golf—"

"And grades and test scores," interrupted Pinkie Pie, who was looking in a different book filled with newspaper clippings, graphs, and student records. "And plays and bake sales and dances and science fairs…"

"They still have to gloat!" said Rainbow Dash. She held up an old school newspaper with a photo of the Wondercolt dressed up like a clown with a wig, a patchwork suit, and a giant red nose.

Sunset Shimmer shrugged. "Seems kind of silly to me."

"SILLY?" Every girl looked at her, aghast.

"It's not like we'll be fighting the powers of evil magic," sighed Sunset Shimmer.

"No," said Fluttershy seriously. "We'll be fighting against a school full of meanies. Not everything has to be magic to be important."

Sunset Shimmer hung her head. Her enthusiasm for magic of all kinds was always getting her in trouble. "You're right," she apologized. "I'm sorry. I know it's a big deal."

"That's putting it mildly, darling," chimed in Rarity. "They're still revamping the playing fields in preparation."

But Sunset Shimmer was confused. "I just don't understand why there's this big rivalry. Aren't the Friendship Games supposed to be about our two schools getting along?"

Applejack held up the photo of the Wondercolt statue pranked to look like a clown. "It's kinda hard to get along with someone who beats you at everything."

"Well, not anymore," Rainbow Dash announced, determined. "This time, things are gonna be different." Rainbow Dash did not like to lose—at anything.

"What do you mean?" asked Sunset Shimmer.

A sly smile turned up the corners of Rainbow Dash's mouth. "Oh, you'll find out," she said playfully. Rainbow Dash beamed at her friends mysteriously. What was she up to?

CHAPTER

4

Game Plan

★ ★ ★

Principal Celestia and Vice Principal Luna were standing behind a podium at the front of the gymnasium. All the Canterlot High students were in the bleachers, including the Equestria Girls.

Principal Celestia cleared her throat and spoke into the microphone: "As I'm sure you know, tomorrow Canterlot High will be hosting our fellow students from Crystal Prep Academy."

Kids groaned, booed, and sighed. Nobody looked very excited.

"We join together," continued the principal, "in the spirit of excellence, sportsmanship, and fidelity to compete in the Friendship Games."

One or two kids clapped halfheartedly.

Principal Celestia ignored her audience's lack of enthusiasm and forced herself to smile. "Now, since the Games only happen every four years, I'm sure you're all curious about what goes on...."

"You mean other than us losing?" Flash Sentry shouted from the stands.

The principal glared at Flash. "That

is exactly why I've asked Rainbow Dash to come up and give us all a little . . . context."

Rainbow Dash hopped down from the bleachers and strode to the podium. "Thanks, Principal Celestia," she said. "I know a lot of you might think there's no way we can beat a fancy school like Crystal Prep at anything."

"Unless it's losing to Crystal Prep!" shouted Pinkie Pie. "We're really good at that."

Rainbow Dash ignored her. "I know that Canterlot High has never won the Friendship Games even once."

Rarity sighed, whispering to Sunset Shimmer, "Oh dear, I hope this speech isn't meant to be motivational."

Rainbow Dash ignored the mutterings from the crowd. She knew how to unite a team, she knew how to focus them on winning, and she was determined to do it. "Crystal Prep's students are super athletic, super smart, and super motivated, but there's one thing they aren't. They aren't... Wondercolts!"

Someone struck a drum. A trumpet blared. The school band marched into the gym, playing a rousing fight song. Rainbow Dash's eyes sparkled. She began to sing into the microphone, and all across the gymnasium, students joined in. Her determination and enthusiasm were infectious.

"There's other schools, but none can
Make those claims.
Our friendships here at Canterlot
Won't ever stop.
That's why it'll be a snap to win
These games."

DJ Pon-3 pulled a small mixer out of her

backpack and plugged it into a cable at her feet. The music blasted through the loud-speakers. Kids were clapping and cheering.

Up at the podium, Rainbow Dash was leading the crowd, singing and dancing.

"We'll always be Wondercolts!
From now until the end!
It's a wonder you don't know that.
It's no wonder that we're friends.
It's no wonder!"

The kids in the band headed into the stands, handing out Wondercolt ears and tails for everyone to wear. The Equestria Girls were lifting their knees and tossing their hair, prancing and dancing in time to the music.

Rainbow Dash was grinning.

"We're not the school we were
Before—we're different now.

There's magic in the ties we've
Made that bind.
We're a Canterlot united, and we'll
Never bow.
Together we can overcome all
Obstacles we find."

The walls shook with the roar of everyone singing. The floor shook as the kids danced in the bleachers. They weren't losers—they were the Wondercolts, and Wondercolts knew how to have fun and how to win.

"We'll always be Wondercolts!
From now until the end!
It's a wonder you don't know that.
It's no wonder that we're friends.
It's no wonder!"

Rainbow Dash held the microphone to her lips and began rapping, *"And if some* school thinks that they can beat us, they'll just learn you can't defeat us!"

Pony ears poked up through Rainbow Dash's multicolored hair. Her pony tail began to swish and wave. Wings sprouted on her back, and she flew up over the crowd. "When we walk these halls, we are royalty. Hearts filled with pride and loyalty!"

Kids pumped their fists in the air. They cheered. They smiled. They were ready because they were the Wondercolts.

Fluttershy was thrilled. "That was amazing. Even I feel like we can win."

"I feel like my school pride is at an all-time high," agreed Rarity.

Applejack was thinking about something, however. "Is anybody else wondering how Dash ponied up without playing her guitar?"

"I know, right?" Rainbow Dash had

rejoined her friends and couldn't believe it, either. "It's probably because I'm so awesome."

"Maybe," answered Sunset Shimmer, who was trying to put it all together. "I mean, you *are* awesome, but there's gotta be more to it than that, don't you think? It just seems so random."

"It would be nice if you could get a handle on it." Vice Principal Luna had joined them, and she didn't look pleased. At all. "We'd like to keep magic as far away from the Friendship Games as possible. We don't want to be accused of cheating."

"We don't need magic to defeat those hoity-toity Crystal Preppers!" exclaimed Rarity.

"Totally!"

"Yeah!"

Kids all around them chimed in, agreeing.

"Still, the Friendship Games are serious business," the vice principal reminded them. "We don't want any surprises, especially the kind that could cause us to forfeit. Sunset Shimmer, you came here from a world of magic. Perhaps you can get to the bottom of our magical development."

Sunset Shimmer was both startled and pleased. "I'll do my best."

"Sounds good," said Vice Principal Luna.

As soon as she was gone, Rainbow Dash turned to her friends. "Okay, anybody have any guesses what the events are going to be?"

Pinkie Pie's eyes widened. "Pie eating? Cake eating? Pie-cake eating?"

"They won't even let us see what they're doing to the field. You'd think they'd at least tell the competitors what they're competing in," said Applejack.

"It could be anything," Fluttershy realized.

"Anything?" Rarity was alarmed. "How will I ever pick the right outfit?"

Sunset Shimmer was distracted by something, something she couldn't figure out, and as one of the smartest kids at Canterlot High, she could usually figure out *everything*. "I really want to help," she said to the other girls. "But I think I better go focus on why Rainbow Dash ponied up. See ya later!"

The girls stared at her as she exited the gymnasium by herself.

Pinkie Pie was the first to speak. "Seems like she's got everything under control. Nothing to worry about."

But Sunset Shimmer didn't share her confidence. In the library, she took out her magic journal and dashed off another letter to Twilight Sparkle.

Hey, Twilight, she wrote. *Haven't heard back from you yet. I guess you must be pretty busy with your role as princess, but I could really use your advice right now. You see, I have been given the job of keeping magic under control here at CHS, even though I still haven't quite wrapped my head around it, and now, after seeing Rainbow Dash pony up the way she did, it makes me think our magic might be changing. Everyone is looking to me to figure things out and I really don't want to let them down, but I am not sure I have enough experience with friendship magic to solve this....*

She put down her pen and sighed. Hopefully, she would hear back from Twilight Sparkle before the Friendship Games started. Why wasn't she answering her?

CHAPTER

5

She's got game

★ ★ ★

A bell rang, and students in plaid uniforms with the Crystal Prep crest on their red jacket lapels rushed through the halls to class. Twilight Sparkle wove in between them.

"Sorry!" she apologized as she brushed past a group of girls. "Pardon me."

Girls rolled their eyes as she hurried past. Crystal Prep was a very prestigious school, but it wasn't always the friendliest place to be a student. In fact, the kids weren't just determined to beat other schools, they were cold and competitive with one another. Twilight Sparkle was one of the very best students at Crystal Prep, but not always the happiest. The hardest part of her day was when she wasn't in the classroom or the library.

Twilight Sparkle raced up a flight of stairs, down a corridor, and burst through the door of her bedroom. She tripped over her dog, Spike, and he tumbled into the trash can. Twilight Sparkle leaned against the door, at last able to relax. "Spike!" she called. Where was he?

With a cheerful yap, Spike scrambled

out of the trash can and hopped onto Twilight Sparkle's desk.

"There you are!" exclaimed Twilight Sparkle.

Her beloved pooch gave an excited bark, wagged his tail, and covered Twilight Sparkle's face in kisses.

"Okay, okay." She giggled, already feeling better.

Twilight pulled open her desk drawer and took out her laptop. From her pocket, she removed the small electronic device she had activated and plugged it into her computer. Data whizzed across the screen. Twilight Sparkle watched, excited.

She turned to Spike. "Last night's field test confirmed it," she explained. "With this device, I can track and contain the bizarre energy coming from Canterlot High."

Spike growled.

"I know you don't like me going over there, but I just couldn't wait. And soon I'll have all the time I need." She closed her computer and went to lie down on her bed. "All of Crystal Prep is going to be there for the Friendship Games. I just hope all that rivalry nonsense doesn't get in the way of my research."

Twilight Sparkle reached under her bed and pulled out a thick file of scientific-looking papers. "If I can collect enough data on these EM frequencies, I should be able to extrapolate the waveforms and determine their origin. That would practically guarantee my admission to the Everton Independent Study Program."

Spike tilted his head, confused by all the

big words. But he did know that Twilight really wanted to advance her studies on her own.

Someone knocked at the door, and Twilight quickly shoved her papers under the bed. She opened the door, and Dean Cadance spotted Spike. She shook her head. "Twilight, you know the rules against pets."

"Spike isn't a pet," Twilight explained. "He's the focus of my research project 'Human-Canine Cohabitation: Its Effects and Implications.'"

She blinked her eyes innocently, but Dean Cadance wasn't fooled. "If you say so, but Principal Cinch is highly allergic, so I suggest you put on a clean shirt." She plucked a dog hair from Twilight's jacket.

"Why?" asked Twilight.

"Because she wants to see you," the dean answered. "Get changed and meet me in her office."

"Maybe she has news about my application to Everton!" Twilight Sparkle said.

The dean looked concerned. "I've been meaning to talk to you about that. Are you sure that's what you really want?"

"Why wouldn't it be?" Twilight Sparkle asked. "A program that allows me to focus all my attention on my own advanced math and science projects! What a dream come true."

"But there aren't any classrooms with other students," Dean Cadance reminded her. "You'll be doing everything on your own."

Twilight Sparkle grinned. "That is why it's called an independent study program."

"I just don't want you to miss out on anything. That's all. Being around other people isn't a bad thing. Sometimes it's how you learn the most about yourself," Dean Cadance said gently.

Twilight Sparkle shrugged, thinking of the unfriendly students she had passed in the hall just moments earlier. "I guess."

Dean Cadance sighed. "Meet you in Principal Cinch's office in a few minutes."

When the door was shut behind her, Twilight was perplexed. "What's she so worried about? Everton is exactly what I need right now. It's not like I have anything left to learn at Crystal Prep."

Twilight Sparkle slipped through the halls, avoiding as many of the other kids as she could. Twilight opened the door to the dark, wood-paneled office of the principal. There was a thick rug on the floor, serious-looking paintings of serious-looking people on the walls, and a high-backed chair in front of the principal's desk, which Twilight sat down in. A clock ticked and chimed.

Shining Armor entered the room. His dark hair was brushed off his face, and he looked particularly handsome.

Twilight Sparkle was surprised. "Why is my brother here?" she asked Dean Cadance.

Dean Cadance smiled shyly at Shining Armor. He smiled back at her.

Dean Cadance cleared her throat. "Principal Cinch thought that he could, as an alumni, provide some unique perspective—"

"Perspective on what?" interrupted Twilight Sparkle.

"Why, the Friendship Games," announced

Principal Cinch, appearing through another door and taking a seat at her desk. "You competed in the Games, did you not, Shining Armor?"

"I did," he acknowledged.

"And do you happen to recall who won?" the principal asked.

Shining Armor burst out laughing. "Crystal Prep did. We always win."

The principal nodded her head and repeated his words: "We always win."

Twilight Sparkle couldn't figure out what was going on. "Principal Cinch, why did you ask to see me?"

The principal gestured to a glass case filled with trophies and plaques and medals. "Twilight, I'll be honest. It doesn't matter whether or not Crystal Prep wins or loses. The important thing is that we are expected to win because Crystal Prep has a reputation. And it is that reputation, *my* reputation, that is responsible for everything we have here." She gestured out the window at the beautiful grounds, the stately buildings, the pristine athletic fields. "You've done quite a lot, haven't you?"

Twilight blushed. "I don't know. I guess."

"Don't be modest," said Principal Cinch. "You're the best student this school has ever seen. But what I can't understand is why my best student wouldn't want to compete."

"In the Friendship Games?" Twilight Sparkle was baffled. The games had nothing to do with academic excellence.

"Look, Twily," said her brother, resting a hand on her shoulder. "I know it's not really your thing, but representing the school is kind of a big deal. Plus, they could really use your help."

"It seems," explained the principal, "that Canterlot High is undergoing something of a renaissance. Test scores are up, grades, even athletics are on the rise. You see, they are developing something of a reputation." Principal Cinch's eyes narrowed. "This. Cannot. Happen."

Twilight Sparkle shook her head. "I can't possibly participate in the Games; my work is—"

"Ah yes," the principal interrupted. "Your work. Cadance, could you and Shining Armor find my contact sheet for the Everton Independent Study Program?"

Dean Cadance nodded. Shining Armor opened the door for her awkwardly, blushing.

When they had left, Principal Cinch leaned closer to Twilight Sparkle. "I understand you've applied for admission. You see, one of the advantages of having a reputation is a certain amount of influence in such things. So let me offer you a deal. In return for contributing your agile mind to these Games, I will use my influence to guarantee your application is approved." She leaned back in her chair, smiling. "Though I suppose I could also have it denied."

Twilight Sparkle was stunned. She had no idea what to say.

But Principal Cinch knew she had Twilight right where she wanted her. "What do you think I should do?"

Twilight Sparkle was overwhelmed. What should she do? She wanted to get into the program more than anything—but the last thing she wanted to do was join the other kids in the Friendship Games. There really wasn't a choice. She would do what she had to.

Principal Cinch gloated triumphantly. Crystal Prep would win again!

CHAPTER

6

A Losing Game

★ ✦ ★

Twilight was packing for the Friendship Games back in her room and trying to convince herself that this wasn't going to be the worst experience in the whole world. Spike grabbed at a sweater she had put in her suitcase and pulled it out.

"Come on, Spike!" Twilight sighed. "I was

always going to go to Canterlot High for the Friendship Games. The only difference now is that I have to compete. Besides, it's not like Principal Cinch gave me much of a choice."

Spike growled. Twilight Sparkle took the sweater back from him.

"I know. I don't like it, either. I probably won't be able to collect anywhere near as much data as I thought." She looked at the device attached to her computer. Instantly, she brightened. She had an idea. "Maybe I can still get some...."

Twilight Sparkle rummaged through her jewelry box and fastened the device to one of her necklaces. It looked like a large pendant. She grinned as she put it on. She grabbed her suitcase and headed for the door. Spike whimpered.

"I wouldn't leave without you," said

Twilight Sparkle reassuringly. "Just remember to be quiet. And try not to shed." She opened up her backpack. Spike hopped in. Twilight zipped the bag and headed downstairs to the waiting buses.

There were two buses in front of the school—one a regular school bus and the other a sleek tour bus.

"Dean Cadance?" Twilight asked. "I'm not really sure where to go."

Two girls waiting to get on board glared at her.

"You could try the end of the line," whispered Sour Sweet. Her neat ponytail was held in place by a pea-pod-shaped clip.

"What did you say?" asked Twilight.

Sour Sweet smiled insincerely. "Just that someone as smart as you should definitely go first. Right, Sunny Flare?"

She turned to her friend beside her.

"Absolutely, Sour Sweet," the girl answered, a hint of sarcasm in her voice. "On the other hand, you could try waiting in line like everyone else."

Twilight was embarrassed. It seemed like she was always saying the wrong thing. "I-I didn't mean to..." she stuttered. "I was just asking..."

Dean Cadance checked a name off her clipboard. "This is the right bus, Twilight. Go 'head."

"But...I didn't mean to cut," stammered Twilight.

Sunny Flare and Sour Sweet rolled their eyes at each other.

"It's too late now," said Sour Sweet under her breath.

Twilight picked up her suitcase and

her backpack and headed onto the bus. It helped to know Spike was with her, even if no one else could see him. As she looked for a seat, a girl with flaming orange hair and a smattering of freckles across her nose grabbed her arm. "Are we gonna win?"

Twilight threw up her hands. "I don't know."

"Wrong answer!" exclaimed the girl, horrified. "Try again. Are we gonna win?"

Twilight gulped. "Um...I guess. I'm sorry. It's just that..." Twilight looked at the bus full of kids, shaking their heads, snickering, and whispering about her. "I mean, I heard that Canterlot High is doing well...with their reputation...and I mean, it's not better than ours, of course, but we can't let them do it. You know? Win, I mean. Right?"

Kids were looking at her like she was a lunatic.

"You're gonna have to take a seat," said the bus driver. Twilight Sparkle was holding up the line.

But there was nowhere for Twilight Sparkle to sit. Kids put their backpacks on the empty seats or stretched out their legs or made it clear by glaring at her that the girl who didn't think they were going to win was not welcome, not welcome at all, to sit with them.

Finally, she found a place in the way back next to a girl with yellow hair who was listening to music and hadn't heard what she'd said. The girl across the aisle was staring at her. "Hi, Sugarcoat," Twilight said, trying to be nice.

Sugarcoat stared at her, expressionless. "That was a really bad speech. You should consider not speaking in public."

Twilight wished she could disappear. At least she had Spike with her. She pulled her backpack onto her lap and unzipped it just enough to peek in at him. Spike nuzzled her hand but began whimpering when the blond girl beside Twilight Sparkle started rocking out to her music. Spike put his paws over his ears.

"Oh man!" The blond girl grinned. "You have got to hear this!" She pulled out one of her earbuds and stuck it in Twilight Sparkle's ear.

Twilight's eyes widened, horrified by the loud, crazy music.

She closed her eyes and thought about her independent study. She could endure this. She had to. It was her only way out of Crystal Prep—and she had to get out.

CHAPTER 7

Fun and games

✳ ✳ ✳

The Sonic Rainbooms were practicing in the music room. They were just finishing a song, and they had ponied up. Their manes were flouncing, their pony tails were swinging, and their pony ears poked through their hair. Rainbow Dash strummed her guitar for one last mighty note. They sounded better than ever.

"I hope the Friendship Games have a music competition," she said. "Because we would totally rock it!"

As the last strains of the music faded away, the girls' pony features disappeared. "We're supposed to keep magic out of the Friendship Games," Fluttershy reminded them.

"Easier said than done, darling," noted Rarity. "I'm sure in Equestria, magic does whatever you want, but..."

"This isn't Equestria," completed Sunset Shimmer. She was actually from the magical land of ponies. Every now and then, she still missed her old home.

"Well, when it comes to magic, I'm sure

you'll figure it out," said Applejack to Sunset Shimmer. "Even if it's how to turn it off."

"Yeah!"

"Totally."

All the girls agreed. Since their trouble with the Sirens, they had all come to trust Sunset Shimmer—and to count on her. Sunset Shimmer was pleased.

"And while Sunset works on keeping magic out of the Games, I've been working on what to put in!" announced Rarity. She pulled a rack of clothes into the center of the room.

"Rarity, what did you go and do?" wondered Applejack.

"I had a little time on my hands," Rarity explained. "And since we don't know what the Friendship Games' events are...I made a few options for uniforms!" She held up one of her latest designs.

"You really didn't have to do that," said Rainbow Dash.

Rarity grinned. "I know." But she also knew the girls couldn't resist trying on her fabulous fashions. There were special soccer outfits that looked just like what the players wore at the World Cup. There were baseball uniforms, cowboy costumes, and even judges' robes in case someone was a judge instead of a player. Rarity had thought of everything.

Now, if only they knew what they were going to be doing in the competition. That was the big surprise.

CHAPTER

8

Two Can Play at That Game

★ ★ ★

Principal Celestia and Vice Principal Luna were waiting outside the school when the buses from Crystal Prep arrived. Principal Cinch could barely hide her disdain when she shook the hands of the administrators. She wrinkled her nose when Principal

Celestia offered to show her all the new improvements and changes to the school.

"Oh yes." She smiled with forced politeness. "I'm sure that would be . . . fascinating."

Vice Principal Luna smiled at Dean Cadance. "It's always a pleasure to see you," she said. "Even if it means another defeat."

"Thank you, but I hear it's not going to be so easy this time."

As the Crystal Prep students filed off the bus, they checked in with Dean Cadance. Indigo Zap cut in front of Twilight Sparkle. "Coming through," she said, pushing her aside.

"Oh, sorry," said Twilight Sparkle. She took a step backward and bumped into Sunny Flare and Sour Sweet.

"Seriously?" sneered Sunny Flare, irritated.

"Oh! I'm sorry," Twilight Sparkle apologized. "I didn't mean to…Why don't you two go ahead?"

Sunny Flare rolled her eyes as both girls stepped in front of Twilight Sparkle.

"You are such a sweetie," hissed Sour Sweet maliciously. "I am watching you."

Twilight stood there, confused. This was the one thing she was no good at—getting along with the other girls. Lemon Zest executed a perfect backflip from the bus steps and landed beside her. She blasted her music and strutted past Twilight, paying her no attention whatsoever.

"You are kind of a doormat," said Sugarcoat.

Twilight Sparkle felt worse than ever. Sugarcoat, too, stepped in front of her.

Twilight Sparkle found herself at the end of the line. There was nothing to do but wait.

Except that her necklace, or rather the device attached to it, had started to buzz. Twilight Sparkle snapped it open. Making sure that no one was watching her, Twilight ducked behind the statue of the Wondercolt.

She checked her device again. Its lights were flashing brighter than ever. Twilight Sparkle had to find out what it meant. Ignoring the line of Crystal Prep students and the check-in with Dean Cadance, she headed toward the steps into the high school.

Canterlot High students greeted her with hellos and friendly waves, but she didn't even notice. She had to find out what was going on. Her eyes on her device, she followed the glowing arrow down the hallway.

She passed a crowd of kids standing around their lockers.

Cecil couldn't believe it was Twilight. "Hey, Twilight!" he called out.

Twilight hesitated. How did the kids at Canterlot High know her name? It was strange. A throng of students walked past her, all smiling and greeting her.

"'Sup, Twilight!"

"How are you?"

"Hey! What's going on?"

Twilight was very confused. These were the friendliest kids she had ever met— much friendlier than her classmates at Crystal Prep.

A good-looking blue-haired boy stopped in his tracks when he saw her. "Twilight?" exclaimed Flash Sentry. He had thought he would never see her again.

Twilight gulped. Who was this kid? "Yeah?" she asked.

"I almost didn't recognize you," said Flash Sentry. He was so happy; he couldn't stop smiling. "When did you start wearing glasses?"

"Um...like, since forever." The boy was standing very close to her. It was making her feel uncomfortable. He was acting like he knew her, like they were old friends.

"So how long are you here for?" Flash asked.

"Just for the Friendship Games," answered Twilight.

"Right!" Flash grinned. "Of course! We'll totally win with you here."

Twilight's device began buzzing, and she used that as an excuse to escape from the boy. He seemed a little crazy. "Gotta go!" she said, and dashed off toward the stairs.

Flash was surprised. "Okay."

What had happened to Twilight? It was like she was a different person.

CHAPTER

9

Ahead of the game

★ ✦ ★

Rarity was having the girls try on different outfits for the Friendship Games in the music room. She zipped around, pinning a hem here and taking a measurement there. She put Fluttershy in a hockey goalie's uniform with knee and elbow pads and an enormous helmet. Rainbow Dash was wearing an old-fashioned policeman's uniform. Applejack was ready for the tennis courts.

"These outfits are great," said Applejack. "But why would you put so much time and effort into clothes we might not even wear? You're gonna exhaust yourself before the Games even start."

Rarity waved her hands as if it were no bother. "Don't be silly, darling. Putting effort into clothes is what I live for, and spending time on my friends just fills me with energy!"

Out of the blue, for no reason at all, without anyone playing any music or singing, Rarity began to pony up. Her pony ears appeared and her pony tail swished down her back.

The girls were stunned. Nothing like this had ever happened before.

Rarity began rising off the ground. She was floating! Maybe she was about to fly.

Sunset shook her head. "And magic, too?" What was happening to Rarity? Shimmers of purple energy were radiating from her body.

Slowly, Rarity began to return to the ground as the girls watched, amazed. She seemed suddenly very, very tired. "I suppose I could use a break," she said. She lay right down on the floor, exhausted.

Sunset Shimmer was trying to figure out what was going on. She was a bit of a magical investigator. While the other girls crowded around Rarity, she followed the purple energy swirls toward the door. It was almost as if there was something on the other side pulling the energy toward it.

She swung open the door—and there was Twilight!

Nobody could believe it. "Twilight?" they all exclaimed together.

"Yes?" said Twilight. How did these girls know her name?

"Well, I'll be," said Applejack. "You shoulda told us you were coming!"

"Darling, those glasses..." worried Rarity. "And what are you wearing? It's so severe."

Twilight looked down at her red blazer and her plaid skirt. "My uniform?"

"Your uniform for what?" asked Fluttershy.

"For Crystal Prep," Twilight Sparkle answered. "But why does everyone at this school know who I am?"

"Did you just say Crystal Prep?" asked

Rainbow Dash. There was no way their old friend would be playing for another team, was there?

Spike let out a bark from inside Twilight's backpack.

"Spike!" Rarity and Fluttershy reached for the bag, but Twilight spun it away from them.

Her face was pale with alarm. "You know my dog's name, too?"

Before anyone could answer, Principal Celestia led the principal of Crystal Prep into the music room. "Our music program has especially taken off...." Her voice trailed off when she saw the girls. She couldn't believe it. "Twilight?"

"This is getting ridiculous!" said Twilight.

Principal Cinch stepped forward and placed a firm hand on Twilight Sparkle's shoulder. "I must apologize for the curiosity of my prize student."

"Your student?" Principal Celestia was very confused.

"The smart ones," continued Principal Cinch, "are always curious. I'll return her to check in with the rest of her classmates." As she led Twilight away, the girl looked over her shoulder at the group of friends all staring at her.

The girls were speechless. What was the matter with their friend? What was she doing here?

"I didn't know Twilight had a twin sister," said Principal Celestia.

"She doesn't!" Pinkie Pie had just figured it all out. "That Twilight was obviously the Twilight from this world since it couldn't possibly be the Twilight from the pony world since the Twilight from the pony world doesn't go to Crystal Prep or wear glasses!"

Applejack was trying to take it all in. "Twilight, well, *our* Twilight said there were ponies in her world like us. I guess it makes sense there'd be girls in our world like *them*."

Principal Celestia looked like she had a headache. This was too much for her. She had visiting students, and the Friendship Games were about to begin. "Never mind," she said to the girls, and headed back to her office. She looked out her window at the busloads of students getting settled and saw Principal Cinch talking to Twilight Sparkle.

Twilight was apologizing to the principal.

"I was just following these strange readings," she said, holding up her device. "Actually, they led me to those girls."

"Twilight, what you do in your own free time is of..." The principal's voice trailed off. She'd just realized something! "Perhaps they are trying to confuse you. Perhaps they are trying to lure you away."

"It didn't feel like anyone was trying to lure me away," Twilight answered.

Principal Cinch's eyes narrowed. She was determined to triumph yet again at the Friendship Games. "I don't know what they are playing at, but I can guarantee it isn't to help us win."

Principal Cinch took Twilight Sparkle by the elbow and led her back to Dean Cadance, who was still checking kids in with her clipboard. The other Crystal Prep girls glared at Twilight Sparkle. They whispered to one another and rolled their eyes. Twilight Sparkle could only imagine what they were saying.

She went to the end of the line and studied her device while she waited. Why had it gone wild around those girls? What was going on with them?

CHAPTER

10

game Changer

★ ★ ★

The girls couldn't stop talking about the new version of Twilight Sparkle.

"I can't believe she goes to Crystal Prep!" exclaimed Rarity.

Neither could Rainbow Dash. "You're saying Twilight's gonna play against us? She'd never do that."

"*Our* Twilight wouldn't," said Fluttershy.

"Our Twilight," explained Sunset Shimmer, who was also from the land of ponies, "is a princess in Equestria and an expert on friendship magic, and if she were here, we'd know why magic is randomly popping up at pep rallies and costume changes."

The girls stared at Sunset Shimmer.

"I'm sorry," she apologized. "I'm just frustrated that I haven't heard back from her."

"Maybe it's like you said," suggested Applejack. "She's a princess in Equestria. She's probably got problems of her own to deal with."

Rarity agreed. "We certainly can't expect her to drop everything and pop through the portal whenever, especially if it's to deal with something as minor as a few random pony-ups."

But Sunset Shimmer was still worried. "They aren't minor. Magic came into this world when I stole Twilight Sparkle's crown. It's taken a lot for me to earn everyone's trust. If we have to forfeit the Games because I can't think of a way to keep it under control..."

Fluttershy wrapped a reassuring arm around her friend. "Oh, Sunset! I'm sure you'll be able to figure things out."

"Yeah," Applejack said, nodding her head. "You're the one who figured out what was going on with the Sirens, remember?"

"I guess," sighed Sunset Shimmer. "But Twilight is really the one who figured out what we needed to defeat them."

Rarity linked an arm through Sunset Shimmer's. "Don't you remember, darling? What we needed to defeat them was you."

Sunset Shimmer blushed. She still wasn't used to having friends who supported her and believed in her. "All right," she agreed at last.

All the girls cheered.

"C'mon, guys," said Rainbow Dash, springing into action. "Let's see if we can find out any info on the events and come up with a strategy. You coming, Sunset?"

Sunset Shimmer hesitated. There was something she needed to investigate. "I'll catch up with you all in a bit."

Sunset Shimmer took out her journal and peeked inside. But there was no answer from Twilight Sparkle. She was on her own. Unless she could reach Twilight through the portal of the Wondercolt.

She slipped past the Crystal Prep students

milling around their buses, went over to the statue, and placed her hands on it. Immediately, they stuck to the marble. Streams of purple energy began flowing from her fingers. What she didn't know was that on the other side of the Wondercolt, Crystal Prep's Twilight Sparkle was stuck to the statue, too.

"Hey! Let go!" screamed Sunset Shimmer.

The Wondercolt was glowing brighter and brighter until there was a sudden burst of purple energy that sent both girls sprawling backward onto the lawn. As Sunset got to her feet, she was surprised to see Twilight so close by.

"What did you do?" she asked at once.

Twilight looked down uncertainly at her device. What *had* she done? But before she could say another word to Sunset Shimmer, Dean Cadance appeared at her side, reminding her that she still hadn't formally checked in. She led her back to the group of Crystal Prep students.

Sunset Shimmer watched Twilight Sparkle. She was suspicious. Twilight was up to something. She'd had the same feeling when she first met the Sirens, and she wasn't going to ignore it this time. If only she could consult Princess Twilight Sparkle!

Sunset Shimmer turned back to the statue to reopen the portal. But it wasn't there. It had disappeared. The passage between the pony world and the human world was gone. Sunset Shimmer panicked, searching everywhere for the portal. But it had vanished. "Where's the portal? Where's the portal?" she shouted, her anxiety rising.

But there was no answer from Equestria. Something very strange was going
on, and Sunset Shimmer was going to
have to figure it out without any help from
Equestria.

CHAPTER

11

At the Top of Her game

★ ★ ★

Sunset Shimmer raced back to the gymnasium, where Canterlot High was hosting a reception for Crystal Prep. The kids from the different schools each stood staring at one another across the vast room, not mingling, not getting to know one another. The gym was decorated with streamers and balloons, but it didn't feel festive. At all.

Sunset tried to explain to her friends what had just happened.

"What do you mean the portal's gone?" asked Applejack, scratching her head.

"I mean it's gone! It's closed! It's not there anymore!" Sunset Shimmer was a nervous wreck.

"How'd that happen?" Rainbow Dash wondered.

"I don't know," said Sunset Shimmer breathlessly. "But it had something to do with that Twilight." She pointed across the room to where Twilight was peering at her strange device.

Applejack studied her. "What in tarnation is she up to?"

Twilight was scanning the gymnasium.

She walked backward, holding up her device, and accidentally bumped into a clique of Crystal Prep girls. Indigo Zap spilled her soda. Twilight tried to apologize while the girls sneered at her.

Sunset Shimmer summoned her courage. "There's only one way to find out what she's up to. Leave this to me." She strode across the room and walked right up to Twilight. "What have you been up to?" she asked.

Twilight whirled around, startled. "Me? What? Oh, I'm just…"

Indigo Zap stepped in front of Twilight and glared at Sunset Shimmer. "Who wants to know?"

"Um, we do," said Rainbow Dash, who had joined Sunset Shimmer.

"All right, everyone," said Applejack in a

soothing voice. "Let's not get too competitive before the Games even start."

Sugarcoat, who had been sitting across the aisle from Twilight on the bus, spoke up. "The games aren't really competitive since we've never lost."

Fluttershy's eyes widened. She couldn't believe someone would say something so unkind. "That's not a very nice thing to say."

"Sorry, dearie," sneered Sunny Flare, "but these Games aren't about being nice."

"You might use a little tact," said Rarity.

Twilight watched the Crystal Prep girls trying to intimidate the Canterlot High kids with resignation—until she realized that the cheerful girl with pink hair was smiling at her.

"Hi, I'm Pinkie Pie," she introduced herself.

"Oh," said Twilight, surprised by her friendliness. "Hi. I'm Twilight."

Pinkie Pie giggled. "I know. You look just like my friend. Her name is Twilight, too."

Twilight was taken aback. "That's weird." Her device began buzzing again.

"What's that?" asked Pinkie Pie.

Twilight popped open the device's lid. It was whirring and going crazy. "It's sort of a spectrometer," she explained. "I built it to track EM frequencies, but it can also contain anomalies."

Pinkie blinked, completely lost.

"It measures things," Twilight added helpfully.

"Like the party?" bubbled Pinkie Pie.

Twilight looked around the room at the kids standing awkwardly in small groups. "This doesn't look like much of a party to me."

"I know!" agreed Pinkie Pie. "Something is definitely missing. Come on!" She grabbed Twilight's hand and led her toward the bleachers.

Meanwhile, Principal Celestia had stepped up to the podium at the front of the room. She checked her microphone. "Hello, everyone. I'd like to take this opportunity to greet all our visitors from Crystal Prep Academy and welcome them to Canterlot High."

A few kids applauded while the principal continued her welcome speech.

Pinkie Pie showed Twilight two large boxes hidden under the bleachers.

"What in the world are these?" Twilight asked as Pinkie Pie enlisted her help dragging them out.

"Party cannons, of course!" squealed

Pinkie Pie. She threw open the lid of the box to reveal a glittering array of noisemakers.

"And lastly," said Principal Celestia, "I would like to recognize the twelve students that Canterlot High has elected to compete. I don't think we could have chosen a better group to represent the excellence, sportsmanship, and friendship the Games stand for."

Spotlights swung around the gym picking out Sunset Shimmer, Fluttershy, Flash Sentry, Trixie, Lyra, Bonbon, Cecil, Poindexter, Rainbow Dash, Applejack, Rarity, and Pinkie Pie.

Pinkie Pie was in the midst of switching a tray of sandwiches for cupcake platters. She waved quickly before whizzing up a ladder to hang a disco ball. Next, she ran over to DJ Pon-3 and slipped her a dance mix.

Last but not least, it was time to plug in her confetti cannons!

Twilight Sparkle gulped. "Are you sure this is a good idea?"

"Absolutely!" exclaimed Pinkie Pie. She fired the cannons and filled the entire gymnasium with rainbow confetti! Kids started laughing, eating cupcakes, and talking to one another. Pinkie Pie was very pleased with herself. If there was one thing she really knew how to do, it was throw a party.

As she looked around the room, completely happy, little pony ears poked through her pink hair. Her tail grew and grew. She was ponying up! The next thing she knew, she was floating off the floor.

"Ooooh!" she squealed. "Floaty!"

Twilight didn't notice because she was

so amazed that the kids from both schools were finally getting along. But then her device began buzzing and beeping, and she popped it open. She swept it over the bleachers, and the readings went crazy. What was going on?

Pinkie Pie was surrounded by a shimmering aura of purple that wafted away as she slowly came back down to the bleachers. "Awww," she sighed as her ears and tail disappeared.

She felt unexpectedly dizzy and very tired. "I am party-pooped!" she realized. She reached out to steady herself.

The last of the purple shimmers drifted into Twilight's device. It was spinning and shaking. Twilight saw ripples emerging from beneath the bleachers. She peeked underneath them and saw…a forest and then the town hall from Ponyville! As the ripples vanished, the mirage disappeared.

Twilight's device seemed to stop working. It didn't buzz. It didn't blink.

Principal Cinch entered the gym, surveying the party grimly. She was not pleased. Frowning, she addressed the crowd. "Ahem," she coughed.

DJ Pon-3 turned off the music.

"I'd like to thank Principal Celestia for her…unconventional welcome," said Principal Cinch with forced politeness. "It's been four years since the last Friendship Games, but it feels as though nothing has changed. Canterlot High continues to pick its competitors in a popularity contest, and Crystal Prep continues to field its top twelve students."

With a smug, self-satisfied smile, Principal Cinch gestured toward a cluster of Crystal Prep kids. "It's a comfort to know," she continued, "that even after so many years, your school remains committed to its ideals, however misguided they may be. I wish you all the best of luck, regardless of the inevitable outcome."

Pinkie Pie's confetti covered the floor. A Canterlot High student or two kicked at it, already feeling defeated. No one felt much like partying anymore.

Pinkie Pie was sitting hunched over on the bleachers. Applejack came over to her. "I'm sorry," she said. "I thought your party additions were really swell."

Fluttershy smiled at her. "They definitely broke the ice."

"If only that Principal Cinch hadn't frozen it again," fumed Rarity.

"Yeah," said Pinkie listlessly. "She's awful."

Sunset Shimmer noticed that something was really the matter with Pinkie Pie. This wasn't just disappointment; she seemed sick. "Wow. What happened to you?" she asked.

Pinkie Pie rubbed her eyes. "I don't know. Everyone started having fun after Twilight and I fired the party cannons, and I ponied up...."

"Of course you did," said Sunset Shimmer. It seemed to happen whenever the girls were happy. But what did it mean?

"But then the magic just drained out of me," Pinkie Pie sighed.

"Wait," said Sunset Shimmer, alarmed. "What do you mean *drained out*?"

"Hey, where is the other Twilight?" wondered Applejack.

Vice Principal Luna was at the podium. "Good morning, students. I'm sure you are all thrilled to start the first day of the Friendship Games. Our competitors will face off in every aspect of the curriculum, culminating in the elimination equation finale."

The kids in the gymnasium cheered!

The Friendship Games were about to begin.

CHAPTER

12

Let the games Begin!

★ ★ ★

The first event, the Academic Decathlon, started in the science lab. Kids crowded into the doorway and peeked through the windows to get a look at the competitors.

Dean Cadance was explaining the rules: "You will be scored on chemistry, home ec, and everything in between. But remember, only the six students from each team with the most points will move on to event number two. Good luck!"

The teachers and administrators stood by, scorecards in hand. The school bell rang—and the experimenting began! The Wondercolts and the Shadowbolts lit their Bunsen burners. They picked up their pipettes. They tested their test tubes.

Twilight dripped a solution into her test tube, and it turned from red to blue.

The Great and Powerful Trixie dripped a solution into her test tube . . . and it exploded. When the smoke cleared, Trixie had vanished. Sort of. She was hiding under her lab table.

Sunset Shimmer's test tube went from red to blue, and so did Rarity's and Pinkie Pie's. Flash Sentry's turned black, but at least it didn't explode. A girl from Crystal Prep watched as her test tube bubbled over. The judges wrote down their scores.

In the home ec kitchen, kids slid their soufflés into the oven. Would they rise or would they fall? The Canterlot High team members crossed their fingers but watched, disappointed, as their soufflé went up, up, up, and then flopped hopelessly down. Sour Sweet and Sunny Flare from Crystal Prep produced a perfect soufflé. But Pinkie Pie and Fluttershy managed to create a soufflé within a soufflé that not only looked amazing but also tasted delicious.

The next event was in the wood shop, and each team was working on building a birdhouse. Hammers pounded, drills buzzed, and saws sent sawdust up into the air. Applejack and Rainbow Dash worked together and created an architecturally sound and good-looking birdhouse. Indigo Zap and Sugarcoat made one with two stories, decorated in flames. Lyra and Bonbon's birdhouse kept collapsing. Each judge wrote something in her book. A spelling bee was happening in the auditorium. The competitors all sat on the stage facing the judge, and one by one stood up to take the challenge. Out. Out. Out. One by one, the students were eliminated as the words got harder and harder.

But the hardest test of all was in the math room. Sunset Shimmer and Twilight were dueling at the blackboard. They divided; they added; they erased. They were working on one of the longest, hardest equations any of the kids had ever seen. Twilight kept glancing at her pendant, distracted. She didn't want to be competing in the Friendship Games; she wanted to be continuing with her investigation. Sunset Shimmer was sure that Twilight was up to something. But what? She couldn't think about it. She had to focus on the equation.

Finally, both girls put down their chalk, and the judges swooped in to check over their work. Faces peered in at the window. Kids held their breath. Who would win? Would it be the Shadowbolts again or did the Wondercolts have a chance this time?

Principal Cinch studied Sunset Shimmer's work. Right, right, right, WRONG. "Incorrect," she announced triumphantly.

Sunset Shimmer tried to hide her disappointment. She'd let down her school and her friends.

Vice Principal Luna stepped forward.

"That means the winner of the Friendship Games' first event is Twilight Sparkle and Crystal Prep."

Twilight Sparkle's teammates applauded, but they didn't look any friendlier. The Equestria Girls, however, all crowded around Sunset Shimmer.

"That was awesome," said Rainbow Dash.

Rarity nodded her head. "Truly amazing."

"But we didn't win," said Sunset Shimmer sadly.

"Well," said Applejack, "that was as close to winning as Canterlot's ever been."

After a brief conference, the judges announced the girls moving on to the next round.

Across the room, the Equestria Girls were hugging one another. Twilight wondered what it would feel like to be part of that kind of team. Suddenly, Flash Sentry was standing beside her.

"Congratulations," he said to her. "You were really great."

Twilight blushed. "Um…thanks."

"I kinda knew home ec pretty much did me in," he said, reminding her of his collapsed soufflé. "Hey, has anyone ever told you that you look just like—"

"Excuse me," interrupted Twilight Sparkle. There was something she wanted to say to the Equestria Girls, and they were leaving the room.

"Okay, then," sighed Flash Sentry, watching her go. It was strange. Except for her glasses, she looked exactly like Twilight Sparkle.

CHAPTER

13

Playing games

✦ ✦ ✦

Twilight saw the girls chatting together by the Wondercolt statue before heading off to their next events. Only Fluttershy remained behind. She opened her backpack and began feeding treats to a little kitten she kept hidden there. She looked up to see Twilight watching her.

"Do you want to give her a treat?" she asked.

Twilight smiled shyly. "Guess I'm not the only one to smuggle her pet into school."

Fluttershy laughed. "Not just one." She unzipped her bag all the way, revealing a guinea pig, a bird, and a bunny in addition to the kitten.

"Oh wow," cooed Twilight. "All I have is Spike." She opened her backpack, and Spike stuck out his head.

Fluttershy could not resist. She scratched him under his chin and tickled his ears. "It really is uncanny," she said. "Does he talk?"

Twilight looked at her as if she were insane. "Um. Not that I know of."

"Congratulations on winning, by the way," said Fluttershy. "Though it didn't seem like anyone on your team was very excited about it."

Twilight's shoulders slumped. "No one at my school gets excited about anything they didn't do themselves." Tears welled up in her eyes.

"That sounds awful." Fluttershy reached into her backpack. "Here. Hold this." She handed Twilight her bunny, and Twilight held it awkwardly in her lap.

"Why?" asked Twilight, confused.

"Holding a bunny always makes me feel better," Fluttershy explained.

"That's ridiculous," said Twilight. But the moment the bunny nuzzled her face, she began to grin. "It actually kind of works."

Twilight patted the bunny, and Fluttershy sat happily beside her. It took Twilight a little while to realize how strange this was. "But I'm on the other team and you just lost. Why are you being so nice to me?"

"You looked like you needed it," answered Fluttershy honestly. Fluttershy's greatest joy was rescuing lost animals—and Twilight had seemed lost to her from the moment she had arrived at Canterlot High. Little acts of kindness always made Fluttershy happy. She was so happy, ears poked through her hair, her tail grew, and the shimmering purple aura sparkled around her.

Twilight was stunned. "What in the world is that?"

Twilight pulled out her device. The readings were going crazy. Streams of energy were emanating from Fluttershy. Nearby, strange ripples appeared in the grass, and a mythic jackalope appeared out of that other dimension and hopped toward them. Spike lunged for it, barking, and the jackalope retreated. Spike followed it, disappearing through the ripples. He was gone!

"Spike!" yelled the girls together.

Fluttershy dropped to the ground, stuck her hand right into the strange ripple, and started to fall into it. Twilight grabbed Fluttershy's feet just in time and pulled her out, with Spike in her arms. The ripples dissolved and vanished.

Purple shimmers poured out of Fluttershy and into Twilight Sparkle's device. Fluttershy looked like she was about to collapse from exhaustion. Her tail and her ears disappeared. Spike jumped out of her arms and back into Twilight's.

"Spike, are you okay?" asked Twilight.

"I think so," answered Spike. Something

had happened to him! All of a sudden, he could talk.

Twilight was stunned. She couldn't believe her ears. Was she going crazy? "AAAAAAH-HHH!" she screamed, and ran off.

Poor Spike was freaked out, too, and he ran in the opposite direction.

"Bye," said Fluttershy weakly.

Spike stopped, turned, and started running in the direction of Twilight. "Twilight, wait!" called the dog.

game's up

★ ★ ★

Spike put his nose to the ground and followed Twilight into the high school and down the hallway. "Twilight, come on," he yipped. "Wait for me!"

At last, she stopped to catch her breath. Spike bounded over to her. There was still fear and confusion in her eyes.

"Why did you run away like that?" asked her dog.

"Oh, I don't know," panted Twilight. "Maybe it has something to do with the glowing girl or the hole in space or the talking dog!"

Spike scratched his ear with his back paw. "Yeah," he agreed. "Weird, right?"

Twilight softened. Spike was still her dog, after all, even if he could now speak. "Are you okay? How do you feel? What happened? Where did you go?"

"Hey!" Spike held up a paw. "One question at a time. This is pretty new to me, too."

Twilight picked up her pooch. "Sorry," she apologized.

"All I know is that I chased that pointy rabbit through the glowy thing, and then I was somewhere else." It felt good to be back with Twilight Sparkle. "The next thing I knew, I was back in that nice girl's arms and I could talk. I don't really understand why I couldn't before. It's so easy."

Twilight peered inside his mouth but was stopped from any further investigation by Principal Cinch.

"Twilight?" she said severely from the other end of the hall.

"Quick," whispered Twilight to Spike. "Hide in here!" She wasn't even supposed to have a pet dog, much less a talking one. She opened a locker door, and Spike jumped inside.

"Twilight, who were you talking to?" asked the principal.

Twilight shrugged. "Myself. It's a nervous habit. Were you looking for me?"

Principal Cinch was suspicious. "Indeed

I was. Quite a coincidence that the Canterlot High students moving on to the next event are the same *nice* girls who were so interested in you. Don't you think?"

"I'm not sure," said Twilight, trying to keep her face expressionless.

"Perhaps you should get to know them after all," Principal Cinch suggested.

Twilight was confused. "But I thought you didn't want me to."

"Let's just say I'm covering my bases. Who knows? Perhaps they will reveal to you the secret of Canterlot High's newfound success."

"Spying feels kind of wrong," said Twilight.

"It's your decision," said the principal, looking down her nose at her prize student. "It's not as though your application hangs in the balance." She smiled. "On second thought, yes, it does."

She strode off down the corridor, her high heels clicking against the tiles.

Twilight waited until she'd turned the corner to let Spike out of the locker. He'd heard everything.

"She is awful. What are you going to do?"

"I don't know, Spike," sighed Twilight. "I don't know."

CHAPTER

15

Back in the game

✶ ✶ ✶

The girls were headed out to the athletic fields for the second event. Fluttershy was filling everyone in on the strange happenings around the statue. "All I did was hand Twilight a bunny. Then I ponied up."

Sunset Shimmer was frustrated. "I just don't get it. Rarity's magic came out when she made us outfits, Pinkie's when she fixed the party, and now Fluttershy." She felt like she was looking at a puzzle, and she couldn't find the missing piece.

"Twilight's pendant thing just pulled the magic right out of me. I couldn't even stand up," Fluttershy continued.

"Like me at the party!" squealed Pinkie Pie.

"Or me right before we met Twilight," Rarity added.

Sunset Shimmer stopped in her tracks. "So she's stealing magic," she hypothesized.

Applejack shook her head. "I don't know. She doesn't seem like the magic-stealing type."

"I know," agreed Sunset Shimmer. "But she had something to do with closing the portal. If her pendant can suck up magic, maybe it sucked up the portal, too."

"How?" wondered Fluttershy.

"I don't know," Sunset Shimmer answered. "The only pony, person, or princess who could help me figure this out is completely unreachable now."

"Yeah, she knows everything about magic and portals and portals and magic and magical portals and portable magics," said Pinkie Pie.

Rainbow Dash had to put an end to this distraction. There was another event, and the Wondercolts were already losing. They had to win this time. "Let's just focus on beating the Shadowbolts. As long as this event puts me on a playing field, I don't think we've got anything else to worry about."

The girls reached the top of the grassy rise leading to the fields, and for the first time saw how they had been remodeled and transformed for the Games. In the center of the soccer field was an archery range, around it was a track, and around that was a motocross speedway with ramps and jumps. The girls' mouths dropped open.

"Am I the only one who thinks this is overkill?" asked Sunset Shimmer.

Applejack turned to Rarity. "I don't suppose you made motocross outfits?"

"Don't be ridiculous." Rarity grinned. "Of course I did." She was prepared for everything.

Down on the field, Principal Cinch was reviewing strategy with the Shadowbolts team. "You will race in pairs," she told them.

"Indigo Zap and Sugarcoat will handle the motocross."

"Yes!" Indigo Zap pumped her fist in the air.

"Lemon Zest and Sunny Flare have requested the short track," continued the principal, "and since archery is a standard requirement at our school, any of you should be able to do it."

The entire team stared at Twilight. Twilight squirmed uncomfortably. Equations were one thing, bows and arrows another.

"Twilight and Sour Sweet will start us off," Principal Cinch confirmed.

Sour Sweet sneered. "That's just marvelous. If you want to lose before we even start."

Principal Cinch glared at her. "Given

that Twilight won the last event single-handedly, I have every confidence that she'll be able to pull her weight here." She turned to Twilight. "Won't you?"

Twilight nodded, terrified.

Students from both schools filled the stands. They were carrying banners and posters, and everyone was eager for the event to start. Spike was scampering around, looking for a seat with a good view. The administrators sat in a raised press box overlooking the field.

Dean Cadance stepped up to the microphone. "Welcome, everyone, to the Friendship Games' Tri-Cross Relay!" The dean smiled as the crowd cheered. "In this event, our qualifying competitors will face off in archery, speed skating, and finally motocross."

Lemon Zest and Sunny Flare were wearing sleek in-line skates and body suits without a single fold or pleat to catch the air. In contrast, Rarity and Pinkie Pie were ready for action in helmets and sturdy skates— but not necessarily fast action.

At the starting line for the motocross race, Indigo Zap, Sugarcoat, Sunset Shimmer, and Rainbow Dash were getting onto their dirt bikes. Indigo Zap revved her bike's engine. She was ready to race. Sunset Shimmer gulped, scared.

Dean Cadance cleared her throat and raised an air horn over her head. "If the competitors are ready…"

The air horn blasted, and the girls were off!

Down on the archery field, Twilight Sparkle lifted her bow and arrow and aimed at the target—which began to move. It flipped! It spun! It went up, down, and sideways!

"Each competitor must hit a bull's-eye before their teammates can start the next leg of the relay," explained Dean Cadance over the microphone.

Fluttershy and Sour Sweet were chasing their targets. Fluttershy leaped over obstacles, jumping over a hay bale and grabbing another arrow. She took aim and fired. The arrow sailed through the air and hit the target. Barely. It was not a bull's-eye.

Fluttershy caught her breath and began chasing down the moving target again. She ducked low; she fired; she missed. Finally, she summoned all her speed and raced as fast as she could ahead of the target and waited for it to arrive. She kept her eye on the small red circle. She fired. Bull's-eye!

Sour Sweet leaped up onto a barrel and let three arrows fly, one after another. Every single arrow hit its mark. She didn't get one bull's-eye. She got three!

Sour Sweet winked triumphantly at Fluttershy. The crowd cheered. Twilight and Applejack stepped up to take their turns. Applejack positioned herself on top of a hay bale and tracked her target. Twilight took a deep breath and braced herself against a barrel.

Applejack's arrow flew high, grazed the target, and sent it spinning end over end. Twilight's arrow hit the left edge of her target. Both girls rushed to restring their bows.

Applejack breathed slowly in and out, focusing.

Twilight looked into the stands and caught a glimpse of Principal Cinch staring at her. She couldn't lose her chance to get into Everton. She couldn't. It was the only way she would ever escape Crystal Prep.

Applejack released her arrow. It sent the target spinning. It was a bull's-eye! Immediately, Rarity and Pinkie Pie were off at the track.

But Twilight's arrow hit the target with a dull thwack and plonked onto the grass. The crowd gasped. The Shadowbolt fans jeered. Sour Sweet fumed. Spike scampered down the bleachers and headed toward Twilight Sparkle on the archery range.

"And Canterlot High is off to an early lead!" announced Dean Cadance.

Spike ducked behind a barrel as Twilight put another arrow into her bow. She pulled back the string. She tried to take aim. But she saw her teammates down at the speed track, glaring at her because they couldn't race until she'd hit a bull's-eye.

Twilight released her arrow, but it flew wide of the target.

Sour Sweet leaped up in the stands. "Well, that's just fantastic!" she shouted, enraged.

Fluttershy couldn't believe how mean the Shadowbolts were. "I'm sure glad I don't go to Crystal Prep," she whispered to Applejack.

"You said it," Applejack agreed.

Rarity and Pinkie Pie skated by. "Wheeeee!" squealed Pinkie Pie.

Still, the Shadowbolts couldn't even

take their places. "If Crystal Prep can't hit another bull's-eye soon, they'll be out of this race."

Her hands shaking, Twilight picked up another arrow. She dropped it.

"You're really bad at this!" screamed Sugarcoat.

Twilight Sparkle looked like she was about to cry.

"I can't take it anymore," announced Applejack. She marched over to Twilight Sparkle, picked up her arrow for her, and drew it back again. "You have to stop aiming at the target," she told Twilight.

"Oh, that makes perfect sense," said Sour Sweet sarcastically. "Don't aim at the target. Thanks sooooo much."

Applejack ignored her and focused on Twilight. "You have to stop aiming at where the target is—and aim at where the target is gonna be."

Sour Sweet couldn't believe it. "Yeah, definitely take advice from the person you are competing against!"

Twilight looked torn. But Sour Sweet was always so mean to her and Applejack seemed to be genuinely helpful.

"Do you wanna hit the bull's-eye or not?" asked Applejack.

Twilight nodded.

"Then trust me," Applejack urged. "Take a deep breath, and let the arrow go... right... NOW!"

Twilight let it fly.

The arrow sailed through the air and hit the target effortlessly. Bull's-eye!

Sour Sweet couldn't believe it. Her jaw dropped. She rubbed her eyes.

Spike stood up on his hind legs and cheered. "Yeah! That's my girl!"

Sour Sweet looked down at the dog and rubbed her eyes again. What was happening? She backed away from the talking dog as fast as she could.

The Crystal Prep skaters took off around the track.

Applejack smiled at Twilight. "See? I was just telling the truth."

Twilight wrapped her arms around Applejack and hugged her gratefully. Applejack beamed—and her ears, her mane, and her tail appeared. She was ponying up! She floated off the ground.

Twilight's pendant was pulling on the necklace chain, floating into the air. It was like it had a magnetic attraction to Applejack. The device popped open on its own.

Shimmers of purple haze flowed out of Applejack, and the device absorbed them.

Applejack drifted back down to the archery field, exhausted. She dropped to her knees. She was out of breath. "What are you doing?" she asked Twilight.

"I don't know!" exclaimed Twilight Sparkle.

A vast sea of ripples appeared along the archery range. Green shoots poked up through them. Huge Venus flytraps opened their mouths. They snapped and grasped at targets and poles and arrows. There were thorny, snapping plants all over the field!

What was happening?

CHAPTER 16

Fair game?

★ ✶ ★

Pinkie Pie and Rarity had a good, strong start on the speed-skating track thanks to Fluttershy's and Applejack's expert archery skills. But Lemon Zest and Sunny Flare were already gaining on them. Lap after lap, they zoomed around the track, synchronized and powerful.

"Canterlot High only has two laps to go," announced Dean Cadance. "But it looks like Crystal Prep is making up for lost time."

Rarity glanced over her shoulder and saw the other team gaining on her. She made the snap decision to turn around and start skating backward. She held out her hands to Pinkie. "Come on!" she urged.

The two girls grabbed hands just as the Shadowbolt team started to pass them. With classic roller derby skill, Rarity whipped Pinkie Pie around a steep turn in the track and sent her careening past the Crystal Prep skaters. Pinkie Pie whizzed around the last lap, grabbed hold of Rarity, and propelled her forward. Both girls crossed the finish line at the exact same moment as their opponents.

Cameras flashed. The crowd cheered.

The girls on their dirt bikes revved their engines. It was time to go. The last part of the relay was theirs. They put their feet on the gas and roared down a steep ramp, flying off in a huge jump as high as the stands.

"This is awesome!" called out Rainbow Dash.

Boom! Boom! Boom! Boom! Each bike hit the track and jockeyed for position. Sunset Shimmer steered expertly over a series of moguls, pulling ahead. But just as she turned the next corner, she saw a thick patch of enormous snapping Venus flytraps taking over the track. She jammed on her brakes and squealed to a stop.

Sugarcoat tried to jump over them and landed right in the sharp-toothed mouth of a giant snapper! Her tires popped, and she managed to clamber off the bike and get away just before the Venus flytrap swallowed it. The crowd gasped.

Indigo Zap saw the field of man-eating plants in front of her but managed to use the flytrap chomping on Sugarcoat's bike as a jump. She catapulted herself into the lead, flying out across the field and zooming ahead when she landed. The crowd was stunned.

A giant flytrap loomed over Sunset Shimmer. Its mouth was open and slobbering. Rainbow Dash pulled up and grabbed her.

"Dash, you saved me!" Sunset Shimmer exclaimed.

"I wasn't about to let my friend become plant food. We can still win this," Rainbow Dash said. Inspired by the spirit of teamwork, she sprouted wings, ears, and a multicolored pony tail. The crowd was shocked. What was happening now? Was this planned?

Rainbow Dash flew through the air, distracting the Venus flytraps. Sunset Shimmer managed to pull free her bike. Rainbow Dash tricked the plants into attacking one another while both girls steered around them and got back in the race. Could they catch up with Indigo Zap?

Indigo Zap looked over her shoulder as she weaved between obstacles. The girls were catching up, and she put her pedal to the metal. There was one more jump. She rode higher and higher up the ramp, but just as she was about to fly free, a flytrap grabbed her rear tire.

Another plant lunged for Sunset Shimmer, and one opened its mouth right near

Rainbow Dash. But Rainbow was driving across the ramp right toward Indigo Zap. She flew over the stem of the plant that had caught hold of the Shadowbolt girl. She helped her ride free! She sacrificed her own win for her opponent.

Sunset Shimmer and Indigo Zap cleared the jump side by side, but Sunset Shimmer was just a tiny bit ahead as they crossed the finish line.

Principal Cinch was in a state of shock.

"Canterlot High wins!" Dean Cadance exclaimed. "I think."

The Shadowbolts were not happy. Sour Sweet snapped her remaining arrows in two. Lemon Zest and Sunny Flare ripped off their speed-skating suits. Indigo Zap and Sugarcoat yanked at their bikes, trying to free them from the ferocious plants.

They were not used to losing, and they didn't know how to do it gracefully.

The ripples began to fade, and as they did, the plants withdrew and disappeared. Indigo Zap and Sugarcoat fell backward. Their dirt bikes were suddenly free.

On the motor course track, the girls rushed over to Rainbow Dash and Sunset Shimmer.

"Is everybody all right?" asked Apple-jack. She still felt out of breath from her strange experience of ponying up.

"We won," said Sunset Shimmer. "But somebody could have been seriously hurt. The magic is going haywire, and I have no idea how to fix it."

Twilight Sparkle felt terrible. "Excuse me. I didn't mean for any of this to happen. I just wanted to learn about the strange energy coming from your school. I didn't know that it was magic or how it worked."

"That's okay! Neither do we," Rainbow Dash admitted, pointing at her wings, which were still there.

"Amazing," whispered Twilight. She reached out to touch them and dropped her device. It popped open. Immediately, purple shimmers radiated out of Rainbow Dash and flowed into the device. Rainbow Dash collapsed. One moment, she was fine, and the next it was as if she had just run a marathon.

Twilight struggled with the device, trying to close it. But she couldn't. "I'm sorry. It just started absorbing energy on its own, but I'm not sure how."

"What do you mean you don't know how?" Sunset Shimmer questioned.

Before Twilight Sparkle could answer, huge ripples appeared in the sky above their heads. Through them, the girls could glimpse the cascading waters of a rainbow waterfall. The waters poured onto the girls' heads, and they were soaked. What was going on?

"The device also causes these corresponding rifts to appear," explained Twilight Sparkle. "I don't know how that works, either."

Sunset Shimmer was frustrated. "Is there anything you do know? Like how to get our magic back or how to fix the portal to Equestria?"

"Equestria?" Twilight Sparkle reacted as if she had no idea what the word meant.

"You're supposed to be so smart," said Sunset Shimmer. "But did you ever think that you shouldn't be messing with things you don't understand?"

"But I want to understand!" Twilight Sparkle exclaimed.

"But you don't," snapped Sunset Shimmer. "And worst of all, you put the lives of my friends in danger."

"I'm sorry," whispered Twilight, close to tears. These girls had been so nice to her, but now they were yelling at her—just like the girls at Crystal Prep. How come she could figure out every math problem, but she couldn't figure out how to be a friend? She ran off the field before anyone could see her cry. Spike bounded after her.

The ripples in the sky vanished. The rainbow flood slowed to a trickle and dripped to a stop. Sunset Shimmer felt terrible about what she had said to Twilight Sparkle. She knew what it was like to make mistakes and feel alone. But when she had felt at her worst, after turning into a she-devil and trying to take over the school, the Equestria Girls had not only forgiven her but made her their friend. Now it seemed like Twilight Sparkle needed a friend, too.

Over on the podium, Principal Cinch was outraged. "You can't possibly call that a fair race."

"Principal Cinch," said Principal Celestia, trying to control herself. "We all saw what happened. You can't think that Canterlot High had some kind of advantage?"

"Can't I?" she answered haughtily. "Even without your trained attack plants, your students have wings."

"Ah, one student," said Rainbow Dash, who had overheard them talking. "And I didn't even cross the finish line."

Principal Celestia sighed. "The race certainly had some extenuating circumstances. Perhaps we should end the Games now and declare a tie?"

"A tie?!" Principal Cinch was horrified. "Was this your strategy all along? To force us into accepting you as equals? I think not. The Games will continue, and Crystal Prep will prevail, despite your antics and whatever performance-enhancing regimen your students are on."

Principal Cinch whirled around, collected her team, and marched them off the field.

Sunset Shimmer approached Vice Principal Luna and Principal Celestia. She was apologetic. "I'm sorry I couldn't stop all of this from happening."

Principal Celestia gave her a gentle smile. "It's not your fault, Sunset."

"Isn't it?" Sunset Shimmer hung her head, dejected. "I should know how to control the magic I brought here, but I don't. I let everyone down, and now Principal Cinch thinks we're cheating."

Principal Celestia tried to console her. "You're being too hard on yourself, Sunset, and who cares what Principal Cinch thinks? The only way we can convince her we're not cheating is to lose...."

Was there any way to lose and still win? That was the question.

CHAPTER 17

Endgame

★ ★ ★

The next day was the final event of the
Games. Students from both schools gathered in the quad and eyed one another sus-
piciously. Who would win? Dean Cadance
reminded everyone that the score was tied
and that whoever won the final event would
be the winner of the Games themselves.

Vice Principal Luna stepped forward, a pennant from each school in her hands. "Somewhere on this campus," she announced, "a pennant from each school has been hidden. The first team to find their school's flag and bring it back wins."

"As soon as our teams are ready, we'll begin," said Dean Cadance.

Fluttershy confided to her friends how disheartened she felt. "I don't know about all of you, but I don't much feel like playing these Games anymore."

"But we have to play," insisted the ever-competitive Rainbow Dash. "This is the last event."

"Yes, dear, but it's a little hard to focus with all the magic stealing and portal opening," Rarity said.

"I feel awful about what I said to Twilight," admitted Sunset Shimmer.

"She is actually really nice," said Fluttershy.

Which only made Sunset Shimmer feel worse. She dropped her head into her hands.

"Let's just get through this last event," Applejack suggested. "Let's prove we're not a bunch of cheaters. Then you can go over and apologize. Maybe we can all work together on getting the magic back and fixing the portal."

Sunset Shimmer took a big breath. "You're right. But I don't think Principal Cinch will ever believe we didn't cheat, especially if we win."

"That kinda sounds like her problem," said Rainbow Dash.

Everyone smiled in agreement.

✶ ✶ ✶

At the other end of the quad, however, Principal Cinch was giving her team a pep talk. "I know I am asking you to beat a team that isn't playing fair, but Canterlot High must be made to understand that even with magic at their disposal, beating Crystal Prep is not an option."

"What if they grow wings again?" Sugarcoat asked.

"A fair question." Principal Cinch smiled devilishly. "Though I believe we can now fight fire with fire. I've seen what Twilight's device can do. Containing magical energy is fine, but have you considered releasing it?"

Twilight was confused. "But I don't even understand how it works!"

Principal Cinch raised an arched eyebrow. "But you'd like to. And since our opponents have already used it to stay competitive, I see no reason why we shouldn't do the same. Unless, of course, you have no interest in the Everton Independent Study Program. Though, honestly, I think there's more knowledge packed in that little device than any independent study program could offer."

All the Shadowbolts clustered around Twilight Sparkle, urging her to use her captured magic. Principal Cinch, who knew she'd always been an outcast, encouraged them. They all let Twilight know that they were counting on her...or else. "Unleash the magic," they cheered.

Twilight took the pendant from around her neck. She studied it. What could it do?

All kinds of possibilities began to arise in her mind, things she'd never imagined. What if it really was magic? She realized she was close to the statue of the Wondercolt. What secrets did it contain? "Imagine the things I could learn by setting it free!" she said aloud.

✶   ✶   ✶

In the middle of the quad, Vice Principal Luna called the students to attention. "If both teams are ready…"

Twilight Sparkle's pendant began to crackle. Twilight knew that her team was counting on her. The device lifted out of her hand and floated in the air in front of her. From across the quad, Sunset Shimmer saw what was happening. So did Principal

Cinch. Her eyes narrowed. Was Twilight Sparkle going to release the magic?

"Twilight, no!" yelped Spike.

At the exact moment Dean Cadance and Vice Principal Luna signaled the start of the final event, Twilight snatched the device out of the air and popped it on. A swirling blast of dark energy hit her right in the forehead. Currents of magic crisscrossed through her body. The pendant fell out of her hands as she lifted off the ground. "Help me!" she called.

The Shadowbolts watched in horror as Twilight reached out toward Principal Cinch. "Keep away from me!" yelled the terrified principal, slipping away from her.

Lightning crackled. Thunder boomed. It all seemed to be coming out of Twilight Sparkle! Energy exploded and imploded until Twilight was surrounded by a twirling ball of light that at last burst open to reveal a giant girl with black wings, purple hair, and a glowing, twisted horn emerging from her forehead. Twilight Sparkle had transformed into Midnight Sparkle!

CHAPTER

18

Stop the games!

★ ★ ★

Poor Spike began to whimper. Everyone stared, dumbstruck, at Midnight Sparkle floating above them. She looked into Sunset Shimmer's horrified eyes and cackled, "You were right. I didn't understand magic before. But I do now!"

A powerful beam of crackling energy

shot out of her twisted horn and blasted the statue of the Wondercolt. But it didn't destroy it. Instead, it cracked the statue like a pane of glass. Into one of the cracks, Midnight Sparkle sent another blast—and it opened up to reveal another world. The rolling green hills of Ponyville were visible to everyone.

Midnight Sparkle turned toward Sunset Shimmer and blasted her. Just in time, Sunset Shimmer dove out of the beam. It hit the ground. Ripples spread out across the quad like a fissure in the earth. Students scrambled back from the edge. Rarity and Fluttershy stumbled toward it, and their friends tried to rescue them.

Principal Cinch headed toward the exit.

"Where are you going?" demanded Sunny Flare.

"Anywhere to avoid that monster, and I suggest you do the same!"

Sunset looked at the world visible through the rifts. "Equestria!" she cried.

Midnight Sparkle blasted the statue again, and cracks spread up toward the sky. It was as if the whole world of Canterlot High were falling to pieces. Sunset Shimmer knew she had to stop this, but how? She hurled herself toward the statue. "Twilight!" she shouted. "You can't do this."

"Why not?" Midnight Sparkle cackled. "There's a whole other world right there, and it's filled with magic!" She fired at the sky, and it fell away like a piece of glass, revealing more of Equestria.

"But you are destroying this world to get it!" Sunset Shimmer was begging her to stop.

"So what? There's more magic there,

and I want to understand it all!" She turned her horn toward the statue.

Sunset Shimmer spotted the pendant on the ground and, with all her might, grabbed it. She clutched it tightly with her fingers and raised it up over her head. As Midnight Sparkle released another blast, Sunset Shimmer managed to put the pendant directly in its path to absorb the magical energy. Sunset Shimmer fell backward, but she didn't let go.

Frustrated, Midnight Sparkle focused her power and sent out an even stronger blast—but Sunset Shimmer rolled toward it and caught it with the pendant before it could hit anything else.

"You can't understand everything," Sunset Shimmer warned Midnight Sparkle. "No one can."

"Oh, but I can! Oh, but I will!"

Sunset was struggling to hold on to the pendant filled with magical power, and it flew out of her hand and clattered to the ground.

Rainbow Dash, Applejack, and Pinkie Pie held tight as Rarity and Fluttershy dangled from the edge of the rift.

"Hang on!" urged Rainbow Dash.

"Obviously," Rarity gasped.

The rift widened. Rainbow Dash and Pinkie Pie started slipping toward it. Applejack pulled and strained, trying to keep all her friends from falling in. "Don't let go!" Applejack begged.

All of a sudden, Applejack felt a surge of power. She wasn't alone. She had help. Indigo Zap and all the kids from Crystal Prep were holding on, too, stretching farther and farther, right back to the front door of the school. "We've got you!" said Indigo Zap.

Sunset saw the danger her friends were in and the chain of kids all working together, and she knew exactly what to do. She grabbed the glowing pendant again and turned toward Midnight Sparkle. "This isn't the way. I know you feel powerful right now, like you can have everything you want. I've been where you are. I've made the same mistakes you're making."

Midnight Sparkle's dark eyes glittered. "You're wrong! I can have everything I want!"

"No, you can't." Sunset Shimmer shook her head. She knew what she was talking about. She'd turned into a demonic beast once herself. "Even with all that magic and power, you'll still be alone. True magic comes from honesty, loyalty, laughter, generosity, and kindness. I understand you, Twilight, and I want to show you the most important magic of all—the Magic of Friendship!"

Sunset Shimmer's pony ears appeared and her tail grew long. She'd ponied up—and she was ready to take on Midnight Sparkle on her own terms. From her entire being came a shining aura of sunlight that connected and healed all the rifts and fissures. It touched every student. It even reached to Midnight Sparkle.

Midnight Sparkle fought back against the beam of light, and the air crackled with the opposing currents. But Sunset Shimmer didn't want to fight. She stretched out her hand to Midnight Sparkle.

Somehow the rays of light were getting through to Midnight Sparkle. She began to see the kids beneath her holding hands, and she saw Spike's worried face. The sight of her beloved dog was more powerful than anything. She realized Sunset Shimmer's hand was extended toward her. She wanted to take it.

"Take my hand, Twilight," Sunset urged. "Let me show you there's another way, like someone else once did for me." Midnight Sparkle reached out and clasped Sunset Shimmer's fingers with her own.

With a magical whoosh, all the energy and enchantment poured back into the statue of the Wondercolt. The portal to Equestria was restored—and the world of Canterlot High was back to normal. Midnight Sparkle drifted down to the ground, transforming into Twilight Sparkle once again.

"I'm sorry," she said at last. "I didn't mean for any of this to happen."

"I know," Sunset Shimmer said kindly. "And going on my own experiences, we'll all forgive you."

Spike leaped into Twilight Sparkle's arms and gave her a sloppy kiss.

CHAPTER

19

Everyone's a Winner

★ ★ ★

Principal Cinch was ready to declare victory for her school the moment everything had quieted down. "Principal Celestia," she announced, "on behalf of Crystal Prep, I demand that you forfeit the Friendship Games. Clearly, Canterlot High has had an unfair advantage for some time, and it's certainly obvious that your students have been using magic for their own benefit."

"I'd like to think that saving the world benefits us all," said Principal Celestia with a tight smile.

Sugarcoat stepped forward and spoke up. "At least they didn't manipulate Twilight into releasing all the stolen magic and turning into a power-crazed magical creature that tried to rip the world apart just to win a game."

"Wow," said Pinkie Pie, wide-eyed. "That's a lot to take in when you say it all at once."

Principal Celestia turned to stare at Principal Cinch. Was it true?

"That's ridiculous," huffed Principal Cinch.

But Spike also was ready to speak up. "Nope. That's pretty much what happened."

After everything that had occurred, no one even blinked at a talking dog.

Sour Sweet sighed. "Actually, we're all to blame." Under her breath, however, she added, "But mostly it was Twilight."

Principal Cinch wasn't going to give in. "Obviously, my students have been infected with your magic, but I plan on taking all of this up with the school board."

"Good," agreed Principal Celestia. "I'm sure they would be very interested in hearing all about the magical students with wings."

"And the portals to different dimensions," added Vice Principal Luna.

"And don't forget to tell them about the talking dog." Dean Cadance smiled.

"Because that would ruin your reputation," agreed Spike.

Principal Cinch looked from Vice Principal Luna to Principal Celestia to Dean Cadance and realized that she was beaten. Frowning, she stormed back into the school.

Principal Celestia noticed that all the students were gathered around her. "I know these Friendship Games haven't been what any of us expected, but given what we've all just been through, I think it's fair to declare us all winners."

There were going to be medals and ribbons for everyone!

Everyone cheered—even Spike.

Dean Cadance walked over to Twilight Sparkle. "I guess that was one way to finish up your time at Crystal Prep. Pretty sure Principal Cinch will be fast-tracking your application after all of this."

Twilight wasn't so sure. "I've been thinking about it, and I'm not so sure now is the time for me to apply to Everton."

"Really?" Dean Cadance was surprised.

Twilight Sparkle looked thoughtful. "I may know about a lot of things, but friendship really isn't one of them, and I'm definitely not going to learn more about it by being alone all the time."

"So you're staying at Crystal Prep?"

Twilight bit her lip. An idea had come to her, but she was tentative about speaking it out loud. "Well," she began, "it seems the students here at Canterlot High know an awful lot about the subject. I don't suppose…"

"You could transfer to this school instead?" Dean Cadance suggested.

"Really?" Twilight Sparkle could barely contain her excitement.

Dean Cadance was a little sad, but she

understood. "I'd miss you terribly, but I think that's a great idea. I'm sure I could speak to Principal Celestia about it. She's like an aunt to me."

Twilight and Spike looked at each other, delighted. The next thing to do was tell the Equestria Girls.

They were all clustered around the statue of the Wondercolt. Sunset Shimmer had found her journal.

"Still no word from Princess Twilight?" Fluttershy asked.

Sunset Shimmer shook her head. "Not yet. But I think I figured out how magic works in this world. We pony up when we're showing the truest part of ourselves. I was so busy waiting for someone else to give me the answers that I gave up looking for them myself. I'm sure there will be more magical problems that pop up in this world. Like Applejack said, Princess Twilight has her own problems to worry about in Equestria. We can't expect her to always be around to help us."

That was the thing about magic. You might not understand it, but you didn't have to, really, because whenever friends got together, you could be sure it was going to happen!

Twilight Sparkle approached the girls. "I'm not sure how much help I can be, but I'd like to try. If you would all give me a chance…"

Principal Celestia, who had just finished conferring with Dean Cadance, came over to join them. "It seems we have a new Wonder-colt here at Canterlot High! I'm sure I can count on you girls to make her feel at home."

"You sure can!" Sunset Shimmer promised.

The girls all hugged one another—and Spike, too.

CHAPTER

20

Life After the games

✶ ✶ ✶

A few days later, all the girls decided to have a picnic outside. They spread a blanket in front of the Wondercolt statue and began eating their lunches and catching up with one another. They were just packing up and getting ready to go back to class when Twilight Sparkle, the Princess of Friendship from Equestria, burst through the portal.

She was in a total panic and talking a mile a minute. "I'm so sorry I didn't get here sooner," she apologized. "I didn't get your message until just now because I was caught in this time travel loop and, honestly, it was *the* strangest thing that has ever happened to me...." Her voice trailed off.

Princess Twilight Sparkle had just noticed the new girl sitting with her friends. She blinked. She shook her head. She stared. Twilight Sparkle, the former Crystal Prep student, was equally confused. She gave the princess an awkward wave.

"Make that the second strangest!" announced Princess Twilight Sparkle.

The Equestria Girls burst out laughing. It was good to see their friend again—and there was a lot to catch up on. A lot!

EVERYONE WINS WITH FRIENDSHIP

Every four years, Canterlot High School and Crystal Prep Academy compete in the Friendship Games. There are academic contests, athletic events, and plenty of opportunities to discover how powerful teamwork can be. Turn the page to get started on your very own Friendship Games!

WHO IS ON YOUR FRIENDSHIP TEAM?

Each Equestria Girl shines in her own special way—from acing the spelling bee to hitting a bull's-eye at the archery range. Decide which of your *own* friends would star in each of the following events:

Science Experiments: _____

Cooking: _____

Carpentry: _____

Spelling Bee: _____

Math Challenges: _____

Archery: _____

Biking: _____

Running: _____

MiXeD-uP MaGiC!

When Twilight Sparkle, the Princess of Friendship, visits Canterlot High, she doesn't look like a pony—she looks like a real girl! But there is also a girl named Twilight Sparkle who goes to Crystal Prep. Can you find her? What makes her different from the Princess of Friendship?

WHen WOULD YOU PONY UP?

The Equestria Girls pony up when they play great music together—and when they are doing something that makes them very happy. When do you pony up? Describe where you are and what you are doing when your pony ears and pony tail appear!

_____

_____

_____

_____

_____

_____

_____

DECORATE THE UNIFORMS!

Rarity is working hard—designing, measuring, and sewing—but she needs a helping hand. Can you help her color and decorate these uniforms for the Friendship Games?

BULLieS aND BUDDieS

The Crystal Prep girls are not always very nice
to Twilight Sparkle. They make fun of her.
They won't let her sit with them on the bus,
and they even bump into her on purpose.
Have you ever felt left out, teased, or bullied?
What happened? How did it feel?

_____

_____

_____

_____

_____

_____

_____

_____

Luckily, each of the Equestria Girls reaches out to Twilight Sparkle and offers her the gift of friendship. Can you list ways you could help someone being teased or left out at your school? It can be as simple as a smile or as comforting as one of Fluttershy's pet bunnies!

_____

_____

_____

_____

_____

_____

_____

_____

A Magical Mixer!

The Crystal Prep players are about to arrive, and Pinkie Pie is planning a party to welcome them to Canterlot High!

What snacks should she serve?

_____

_____

_____

_____

_____

What songs should be on her party playlist?

_____

_____

_____

_____

_____

Event #1

The Friendship Games are about to begin!
Unscramble the players. Then draw a line
from each player to her correct team!

YNNSUAREFL

_____

IEPPIEINK

_____

WEESSOTUR

_____

XRTEII

_____

GPKHTTWLEARILIS

_____

MSMNIEUERSSHT

_____

Event #2

Applejack is participating in the obstacle course. Get her to the finish line… but watch out for dead ends!

START

FINISH

Event #3

Test your Pony Power knowledge in the trivia challenge by answering these questions about the Equestria Girls and Canterlot High!

1. Where does Sunset Shimmer come from originally?

   _____

2. What did Sunset Shimmer do that she still regrets—but her friends forgave her for?

   _____

3. What instrument does Fluttershy play for the Sonic Rainbooms?

   _____

4. How did Sunset Shimmer help defeat the Sirens?

   _____

5. How is Twilight Sparkle planning to escape Crystal Prep?

   _____

6. What is the name of Twilight Sparkle's older brother?

   _____

7. How many times has Canterlot High won the Friendship Games?

   _____

8. What happens when the Equestria Girls pony up?

   _____

Answers: 1. She used to be a pony in Equestria. 2. She stole the Element of Harmony—and turned into a she-devil. 3. She keeps the rhythm with her tambourine. 4. She helped everyone get along to harness the Magic of Friendship. 5. She wants to win a scholarship to the Everton Independent Study Program. 6. Shining Armor. 7. None! Crystal Prep is undefeated. 8. Pony ears, manes, and tails magically appear!

THe FiNaL EVeNt!

It's time for you and your friends to rewrite the Friendship Games! Fill in the blanks with your own funny words and see what happens at the track!

The girls on the _____ revved their engines. They
(plural noun)

put their _____ on the gas and _____ down
(noun) _(past tense verb)_

a steep ramp. Sunset Shimmer _____ steered over
(adverb)

a series of _____, pulling ahead. But just as she
(plural noun)

turned the next corner, she saw a(n) _____ patch
(adjective)

of _____ snapping _____. She slammed
(adjective) _(plural noun)_

on her brakes. Sugarcoat tried to _____
(verb)

over them and landed right in the _____
(adjective)

mouth of a giant _____! Her tires popped, but
(noun)

she managed to clamber off the bike and get away!